A Pocketful
of Rye

A Pocketful
of Rye

by A. J. Cronin

Little, Brown and Company · Boston · Toronto

A Pocketful
of Rye

one

THE EXPRESS LETTER came late in the afternoon.

I was standing comfortably with Matron Müller on the terrace of the clinic, putting on my usual act of kindly interest as the children packed into the big green departure coach that would take them through the mountains by the Echberg Pass to Basle for the chartered night flight back to Leeds. It hadn't rained much during their six weeks and the little runts looked well and full of themselves, packing the open side windows to shout *auf Wiedersehen* and other picked-up bits of Schweizerdeutsch. They were waving the paper Swiss flags that Matron always handed out with sample bars of patriotic milk chocolate. As the coach rolled down the drive they began to sing "Lili Marlene." They had picked that up too, endlessly playing the old scratched record in the playroom.

"Well, that's the last batch of summer, Matron," I remarked on a poetic note, as the coach disappeared behind a frieze of firs. "They weren't bad brats."

"*Ach, Herr Doktor.*" She raised a reproving finger, but fondly. "Vy must you use that vort. Brats. These last were goot child-ern and for me a goot child is the handvork of Gott."

"But Matron," I improvised quickly, "brat is just an affectionate English idiom. In Britain people of the highest rank will publicly refer to their offspring as brats."

"Ach, zo? You are serious?"

"I assure you."

"Zo! A fun affection. An English odium of vellborn people."

"Exactly."

Her small eyes approved me indulgently. Hulda Müller was a short, thick woman of about sixty, her architecture late Victorian, with a magnificent portico. Thorny gray hair protruded from her white stringed cap, her faint moustache was discreetly powdered. Draped to the heels in the shapeless white gown to which the cantonal nurses were condemned, she was the genuine Schweizer article. Correct, hygienic, humorless, unutterably dull, and while not, in the cheap sense of the word, a snob, imbued with an inherent Germanic reverence for rank. But capable and industrious, a worker fifteen hours a day, coping with shortage of staff in the ward and the kitchen, feeding me as I had never, in my spotty down-at-heel career, been fed before.

"It is highly agreeable to me that you make explanations of such odiums, Herr Doktor Carroll. You, a person knowing and yourself coming from the *Hochgeboren.*"

"A pleasure, Matron. You'll have all the odium I'm capable of."

Oh, careful, you clown, don't push it too far. I flashed a smile at her, loaded with charm. In any institution it is the first rule of life to be in with the matron. And since my heaven-sent arrival seven months ago I had worked diligently on Hulda, soaping her with some inspired fictions, creating a few noble ancestors to strengthen my image. So now this fire-breathing old dragon, this veteran of the bedpans, this Hippocratic priestess in a white soutane was entirely mine or, rather, I was hers—her bright-eyed *Junge.*

"Now ve have the six veeks' pause," she reflected. "You vill re-commence your postgraduates at the Zürich Kantonspital?"

"I'll go down at least once or twice a week," I agreed thoughtfully. "Beginning on Tuesday."

"Ach, it is goot to have the charge of a young, eager, scientific doktor. Our late Herr Doktor vas . . ." she shook her head, *"ein Schrinker."*

"Das war nicht gut für Sie," I responded, demonstrating my advance in colloquial German.

"Nein, aber das ist ein Problem für seine neue Frau." The law that married doctors were unacceptable at the clinic thus defined, she examined the watch dangling from her bosom. "But now I must go to see for your tea." Moving off she glanced at me archly. "You like perhaps these ramekins I make special for you."

"Matron, they're a dream and you . . . you're a regular 'dreamboat.'"

She giggled, not amused, just pleased.

"Dreambote? That's goot?"

"The best."

When she had gone I suddenly felt annoyed with myself. In her own way she was kind and decent. And shouldn't I be thanking my lucky star to be here? On velvet at last after eight years of mucking around in the worst kinds of General Practice.

When I graduated at Winton University I had taken a voyage to Australia as ship's doctor in a cargo boat, then come back all set for the quick trip to Harley Street. It did not take long to demonstrate the financial and professional worth of a low-grade Scots degree. Who wants you with that, with the dung of the kailyard on your boots, and the porridge still stuck to your chaps? At first a few locums, one in the Highlands with a hard-drinking member of the MacDuff clan, then a short assistantship, followed by another locum in the slums of Winton where, half starved, I worked overtime for an obese old sloth who staggered back from his holiday at Glendrum Hydro loaded with the menu cards for every meal, immediately sat down, still drooling all over his paunch, and one by one read them out to me.

Then came a long assistantship in Nottingham with the vague view to a partnership that was never meant to materialize. But why elaborate the sorry record: the long hours in sweaty surgeries, the night calls, the health insurance cards to be faked after-hours, the

three

DAWN COMES EARLY in the Swiss uplands and on the morning of October 7, although it went against the grain, I was up with the lark to make a quick round of the ward. We had only five cases, none of them serious: two simply retained for observation after pleurisy, a mesenteric adenitis and a synovitis of the knee, the so-called "white swelling," both certainly due to bovine TB, and finally an early Pott's curvature that I had already put in plaster. By half past eight I had finished and after breakfasting and checking with Matron, whom I had already skillfully briefed and who, to my surprise, seemed quite intrigued at the prospect of the new arrivals, I set out for Zurich in the clinic's Opel station wagon. Why so early, Carroll? Why such indecent haste? You are not duty bound to meet and greet the dear pilgrims until half past five. Could it be that there was purpose in that telephone call last night when the good Matron had retired and that once again you are putting pleasure before business?

47

At first the mountain road is steep, winding and narrow, but beyond Jenez it opens out into the Coire valley. At this hour, except for a few farm wagons, there was no delaying traffic. I made good time and was in Zurich, cruising along the Tielstrasse, looking for an unmetered parking place, just after eleven o'clock.

Zurich has been decried as a city of underground bankers. I have nothing against bankers, since I never meet them, and I liked this fine, rich city, presiding over its broad river and the Zürichsee with the dignity of an elder statesman, and never cluttered with gaping tourists, since most foreigners came quite simply to visit their money. A stroll down the Bahnhofstrasse, where I stopped at Grieder's to buy a couple of ties, brought me to the Baur-au-Lac just before noon. I went into the garden and ordered a dry martini. It came at once, substantial and really dry, with a thin curl of well-pared lemon peel, confirming my unbiased award of five stars to this superb hotel. Naturally it is expensive, but now that I had some sort of income I enjoyed blowing it; moreover my visits were infrequent and as Lotte enjoyed everything deluxe it paid off to indulge her here.

She arrived at that moment, bareheaded and smiling, very smartly turned out in a plain but attractive tan suit that exactly matched her corn-straw hair. I should explain that Lotte is Swedish with the coloring of her race, not the conventional slinky fictional blonde, but a big, easygoing, solidly beautiful girl with the athletic body of a champion discus thrower and careless honey-colored eyes that usually seem full of laughter. Of course she doesn't throw the discus. She is an ex-air hostess promoted to receptionist at Zurich for a big Scandinavian charter line—the Aktiebolaget Svenska Örnflyg—and, both being practiced in the art, we had picked each other up in the airport bar about four months ago when I was dispatching a consignment of boys to Birmingham. I had become fond of Lotte since then and except for one thing I would have been mad about her. As it was, I warmed all over as she sat down and crossed her legs under her short skirt. But the waiter was already at my elbow.

"I'm one ahead of you," I said in German. As part of her job she spoke five languages and, teaching it the best way, had brought my German to what might justly be termed top form—we often laughed together over the way I'd had on the committee with my *"Entschuldigen Sie, mein Herr, können Sie mir zeigen wo das nächste Abort ist?"* "Can you cope with a double?"

"If you'll have one."

I leaned forward when the waiter had gone.

"You're looking most unbearably attractive, darling."

"Thank you, sir."

"Been meeting many V.I.P.'s lately?"

"Lots and lots. Dark handsome men."

"Hmm. African or Burmese?"

"No, no, one Italian, one French."

"Ah! A mixed vermouth."

She laughed shortly, narrowing her cat's eyes.

"Really, I'm serious, Laurence. Two gorgeous men."

49

"Liar. Only don't start sleeping with them or I'll break your Swedish neck. Incidentally," I said, with a momentary anxiety, "you *are* free this afternoon? You weren't quite sure last night when I called you."

"What about those medical researches?"

"We'll work on them together."

She kept me on edge for a moment then nodded, companionably.

"Not on duty till five o'clock."

"That's perfect. I have to be at the airport myself then." And I told her briefly I was meeting a patient and his mother.

The waiter had brought two menu cards with the drinks. We studied them in silence, ordered, and half an hour later we went into the restaurant, a glassed addition built out into the garden with the river on one side.

I remember so well that delicious luncheon, the last before my troubles began. We both had the iced cantaloupe as a starter, so golden, so sweetly ripe, and dead ice-cold. Lotte, who never seemed to look ahead, or perhaps had no need to supercharge her vitality, chose for her main course poached turbot with hollandaise sauce and little new potatoes vapeur. I had a thick filet mignon cooked *au point* with spinach and *pommes pont neuf*. We drank two of the best, yet relatively inexpensive Swiss wines, she the light Döle Johannesburger, I the red Pinot Noir, and just enjoying the food and looking at each other, we didn't talk much. Coffee was all we wanted afterwards, and we put it down suspiciously fast.

Lotte's apartment was in a new block in Kloten, quite near the airport. I drove there, parked the car at the rear of the building and was beside her as she turned the key in the door. I knew it all: living room with small kitchen off, bedroom and nicely tiled bathroom, all furnished simply and functionally in modern Scandinavian style and excessively clean. Whenever we entered she drew the curtains in the bedroom, gave me her big warm smile and began with complete naturalness, keeping her eyes on me, to take off her clothes. Soon she was stretched out flat on the bed.

"Come quick, Laurence. It is too long since the last time . . . I want lots and lots of loving."

Stark naked, lit by the filtered daylight, she invited the physical act openly, naturally and with undisguised desire.

Afterwards, she studied my face, so intense, it seemed to amuse her.

"We must have a cigarette." She rolled over, like a big languid cream-fed yellow cat, reaching to the bedside table, speaking in English which she knew moderately well. "Then again we have much more fun-fun."

That, exactly, was the trouble with Lotte. Bliss when we made love, and afterwards nothing. No tenderness, no persistent sense of belonging, nothing of that yearning which springs not from the body but from the spirit. Of course, an excess of yearning could be dangerous: to my cost I had learned how difficult it could be getting rid of a yearner, particularly the soulful type. But surely, I told myself, there should be *something*, a communication of the heart rather than the adrenals, that endures after the intensity of such a union. Was I asking for the moon? In this case, perhaps. The Swedes, I reflected sadly, were known as prolific copulators, they took it all in their athletic stride. A hygienic exercise.

Lotte drew on her cigarette, her mind already diverted to the mundane.

"Who are these people you are meeting?"

"I told you, darling. A small boy and his mother. It's odd . . . Years ago I fancied I was in love with her. Yet in a queer sort of way I almost hated her."

"See you go on hating. No more of the other thing."

"You can bet on that . . . But Lotte, you don't really love me."

"So you want to be loved? Heart to heart. And pink roses round the door."

"Don't jeer, Lotte. I mean something deeper . . . that you can hold on to when you need it . . . when you're not on top of the world."

She burst out laughing.

"When the dog barks at you in your dark street."

Once, misguidedly, I had tried to confide in her. I was silent. Perhaps she sensed that she had hurt me. She said quickly:

"Ah! Love, what is that but meeting trouble? I like you much. We give each other much satisfaction. And I'm not a gold brick."

"Gold digger," I corrected.

She repeated the words, laughed, then put her arms round me.

"Come. We forget love and enjoy each other."

It was quarter to five when she got up and dressed. With my hands behind my head I watched her out of one eye. In the comedy of life nothing is nicer than a pretty girl stepping out of short, clean white pants— you can keep all your tiddy pastel shades. The reverse process, the stepping in, now being enacted, strikes a bourgeois note. Drawing the curtains, shutting up shop. But in her perfectly fitting saxe uniform, the cockaded bonnet not the common saucy touch but elegant, she looked distressingly smart. The afternoon, which had slightly tarnished me, had put a bloom on her.

"We must hurry, or I'll be late."

I sighed and heaved out of bed. My knees creaked. I was no longer young and healthy.

"I do hate leaving you so soon, Lotte. After being so close to you . . . it's a wrench."

She shook her head.

"You are a nice man, Laurence, of whom I am so fond. I never thought for an Englisher I could feel so much. Don't spoil it all with such sentimism."

"Sentiment," I amended sadly. "And I'm Scottish."

I brought the car round to the front entrance and we drove to Kloten. You may accuse me of being over-sold on Zurich when I commend Kloten Airport as the best in Europe—meticulously efficient, immaculately clean, with a first-class restaurant and a snack bar serving the best coffee I ever drank. We each had a quick cup, standing up. Typically, there was no one at the B.E.A. counter, but from the long range of bustling Swiss desks on the other side Lotte came back with some bad news.

"Your flight is seventy minutes late."

"Oh, blast."

She showed all her lovely teeth in an irritating smile. "You must sit and dream of me, *liebling*. With your so tender heart. And I tell you. When your friends arrive I bring them quickly through customs to you."

I went through to the lower bar, found a quiet corner and ordered a kümmel. Suddenly I felt tired and unaccountably depressed. No, not unaccountably—it was the old post-copulative triste. The Augustine tag came to my mind: *Post coitum omne animal triste est.* How true, how everlastingly true! Usually I can ignore it but today I failed to shake it off. Her crack at my secret hallucination had upset me. And what a fool I was, wasting my time, and substance, in fact wasting my life with these frivolous fringe benefits. Lotte wasn't a bad sort, but what did I really mean to her. A partner in fun-fun. And although she wasn't promiscuous, I had a dismal notion that I was not the only one to share her suspiciously broad and springy bed. But this was the least of my sudden dejection. That mood was coming on, that familiar cursed mood, the epigastric syndrome, or if you prefer it, that psychological punch in the guts. For me there was no escape. Never. Even as a backslider I could not escape that sense of guilt. I had been brought up on sin, both varieties, venial and mortal, the latter, if unforgiven, a prelude to damnation. Ah, goodness, that comprehensive word, that ever-elusive state of good!

Oh, cut it out, Carroll. Be your age. You gave up all that truck years ago. And nowadays who gives it a thought? And if you want to argue, hasn't the recent Commission of Christian Churches practically sanctified all forms of premarital sex, throwing in a few self-service practices as extra jam, with three hearty Christian cheers for *Lady Chatterley's Lover!*

With an effort I turned my thoughts toward the approaching meeting, which disagreeable though it might be, was not without a certain mild expectation. Interesting, in a minor way, to see Cathy again and to know if anything of that juvenile regard for me remained. The probability stirred faint memories and, encouraged by another kümmel and a sustaining club sandwich, I drifted back to Levenford, to that eventful day, and the events leading to it, when I had last seen Cathy Considine and Francis Ennis, the day of Frank's ordination.

four

THE SUMMER THAT YEAR had been exceptionally fine, and on that late August morning as I set out from Winton station the sun beamed benignly in a cloudless sky.

The train was a "local" and as the slow journey wore on with stops at several stations, I had ample time to reflect on the event that was bringing me to Levenford. Actually it was an inconvenience for me to make the trip, since having graduated M.B. at the university during the month before, I had signed on as ship's surgeon in the S.S. *Tasman,* a cargo cum passenger liner plying between Liverpool and Sydney, now due to sail on the evening of the day before the ceremony. But I had promised Frank to be there on his big day, although since leaving Levenford to attend the university my communications with him, to say nothing of my visits, had been infrequent. Frank's sudden decision to enter the priesthood, so logical in one sense, had taken me by surprise. He had never spoken to me of a vocation, although I had long suspected it.

I had already surmised that a subconscious aversion to his father's way of life, while never admitted, perhaps never recognized, had deterred him from continuing the Ennis general practice. But he had meant to be a teacher, and had set out to take his M.A. degree at Edinburgh. And beyond all other considerations his future had been centered on Cathy, their marriage was an understood thing, practically preordained. What could have upset the applecart? A sudden call to give himself to God? Perhaps there had been pressure from the everlasting Dingwall. This I was inclined to doubt, recollecting an incident when the Canon, detaining me after one of our Friday sessions, had caught me by the collar and shaken me till my teeth rattled.

"It's you I want, with your good Protestant blood. What use would Frank be on the parish milk round? Put a rosary in one hand and a lily in the other and you're done with him."

Had some deeper psychological reason inclined him toward celibacy? There was the occasion when, during one of our conversations—I was then a three-year medical student—Frank suddenly exclaimed:

"Isn't it disgusting, Laurence, that the organ of procreation should be the very sewer through which half the impurities of the body are discharged?" And how his expression had frozen when I laughed.

"You'll have to blame that one on the Creator, Frank."

"Not blame, Laurie," he said severely. "It was meant. By omniscient design."

He was an interesting conundrum, still open to speculation! For reasons that were unrevealed, and remained inexplicable, Frank had suddenly slipped out of his commitment to Cathy and taken off for the seminary.

The train was late in arriving, and although I put on speed from the railway station to St. Patrick's, the service had already begun as I slid into an inconspicuous seat beside a pillar. From this retreat I had a clear view of the altar and of the two front rows, where I made out among a number of others, Mrs. Ennis, Cathy, and what looked like the entire extensive range of the Davigan family.

This ceremony is always impressive and I admit it gave me a bit of a turn. The sight of Frank, all in white, prostrate in an attitude of supreme subjection, made me feel a bit of a sickening character. Since I'd cut loose from Levenford I had not infrequently been in the same position for altogether different reasons.

After the final blessing I waited outside, the emerging congregation, which was large, milling round me. Aware that I should not immediately see Frank, I hoped that Mrs. Ennis or Cathy might give me some idea of his arrangements for the day. However, it was Dan Davigan who found me, pumping my hand and patting me on the back with the insufferable presumption of a lifelong boon companion.

"Well met, man. I saw you, had my eye on you, as you slipped in. Why didn't you come forward, proper like, to the place I'd reserved for you? I'm a St. Pat's sidesman now, y'understand, and I throw my weight around. Anyhow, here we are, and I've an invite for you. Celebration repast at the Ennises' home for six o'clock. You'll be there?"

"I'll try."

"Oh, but you must, or Frank'll never forgive you. Sure, your name's never off his lips."

Restively, I looked about me. I still hoped to have a word with Cathy, but she was lost in the crowd or had already gone. I had begun to move away when Davigan exclaimed:

"And now I've a message from the Canon. He wants to see you. In the sacristy. Poor suffering soul, he's a done man, due for retirement to the sisters next month. In you go, I'll wait for you."

There was nothing else for it. I had to go. The old autocrat was in a wheelchair, but still erect, with a book on his knee. His eyes, sunken, but still burning in their sockets, unmistakably alive, took me all in.

"So," he said, when he'd finished looking me over. "I'd a notion to see you before they sent me to the scrap heap." Without taking his eyes off me, he felt for his snuffbox from under his soutane, using his good left hand and, still adeptly, inhaled a pinch. "I perceive that you have slipped, Carroll. Badly. It's written all over you."

I felt the blood rush into my face and neck.

"At least you've still the grace to be ashamed of yourself. I needn't remind you it was you I wanted in there. I worked hard on you too. All those Friday afternoons." He nodded sideways. "But, with that slippery Irish side to you, you got away. However, don't think you'll ever escape. The seed is in you and you'll never get rid of it."

There was a pause. I was grateful that he spared me a cross-examination of my faults, and somehow sad and shamed that I had disappointed him.

"I hope you're feeling better, Canon," I mumbled.

"I'm as well as ever I was, except for the use of one flipper, and good for another ten years. I'll have my eye on you, Carroll."

"I've always appreciated your interest in me, Canon, and all that you did for me."

"Drop the blarney, Carroll. Just let some of our Fridays stick."

Another pause. He took up the book. "As a quasi-literary character, notably an essayist, do you ever read poems?"

I shook my head.

"Well, take this. It's a prize they gave me at Blairs many a year ago. I've marked one poem. It might have been written specially for you."

When I took the book he snapped the snuffbox shut.

"Kneel down, sinner." I had to obey. "I'm going to bless you, Carroll, and it's not only the Lord's will, but mighty appropriate in your case that I have to do so with the wrong hand. For before God, if ever you achieve salvation it'll be the wrong way—by falling in backwards through the side door."

As I left the sacristy, horribly discomposed, I realized I had barely uttered a single coherent word. To recover myself I sat down in the now empty church and opened the book he had given me. *The Poems of*

And there is. Matron has copies of your testimonials. I've seen them and they're . . ."

"That's enough!"

"Yes, it would be a nasty word, wouldn't it? False pretenses. Might even be forgery. And what a bother it might get you into with the General Medical Council." While I listened with growing, deep-seated uneasiness, she went on. "Doctors have been struck off for less. I hope that won't be necessary. For you'd need your miserable little medical degree if I sent you back to general practice in Levenford. That's where you belong and that's where you will go if you don't toe the line. You're the one that'll go back to old Dr. Ennis. He's losing his assistant and he'd take you, on my recommendation." She gave me a thin, bitter smile. "I'm going to get a lot of pleasure watching you sweat it out here with that hanging over you."

nine

I BARGED DOWN THE HILL in a state of mind in which rage, resentment and apprehension prevailed over the suspicion that I was dealing with an unbalanced character. Naturally I had left her without a word. I had found it unprofitable at any time to argue with a woman; still less so now with one thrown off the beam by a prolonged stretch of marital frustration. Did she actually imagine I could be yanked out of the best, yes, if you prefer her word, the softest crib I had ever hoped to drop into? I was established at the Maybelle, I now spoke German fluently—there was no need to fake it—and on the two occasions when the committee had visited the clinic they had expressed themselves as fully satisfied with their choice. If the validity of the testimonials was questioned I could explain that I had lost the originals. And hadn't I been foreseeing enough to protect myself against just such a contingency, this threat to my security? The bold Caterina hadn't thought of that one. I was safe. No need to worry, Carroll, my boy. And yet I was worried. There remained with me a sense of something in the background, unspoken, unrevealed, retained, so to speak, for the *Meisterstück.* Curse that German, I meant the *coup de grace.* No, that was nonsense, yes, rot in any language. Get me back to Levenford? That noxious hole in Clydeside mud? Back to another G.P. assistantship, stuffed with night calls and surgery grinds, with an old boozer as principal, who was more or less tight half the time. She was right—it would be hell. But, never. No, not on your bleeding life, Carroll. I would fight it to the last ditch.

Suddenly, as I approached the clinic, I heard someone calling me, the voice immediately recognizable as Matron's. Perched on the rear balcony like a molting hen, she was flapping me in with a towel. Refusing to be hurried, I slowed to a walk, so that she had ample time to come down to the terrace to meet me.

"Ver haf you been, Herr Doktor?" She was practically foaming at the mouth. "*Eine Stunde* almost I am seeking you."

I permitted myself the liberty of a really dirty look, the first I had ever directed toward her.

"Where the devil do you think I've been? I'm surely entitled to a little time off. I've been taking my exercise."

I perceived with satisfaction that she was taken aback. In a modified tone, though still complaining, she declared:

"Your patient is not so good. Much sickness. All his good *Mittagessen* thrown back."

"What! Sick again?"

"Much."

"You did stop his codliver oil?"

She reddened uncomfortably.

"But it is so goot for him . . ."

"Damn it all, I told you, instructed you, to stop it."

She was silent, giving me best.

"Very well," I said shortly. "I'll have a look at him."

"*Jetzt?* Immediately?"

"When I've had a wash. He won't harm just because he's had a vomit."

This was merely to keep Hulda in her place. When she was out of sight I went across to the guest chalet.

He was lying fully dressed, on his bed, with his eyes on the ceiling. Beside him an enamel basin seemed to contain most of his lunch, but it gave out no stink of fish oil. One hand was placed protectively on his stomach. He removed it quickly as I came in, an action I did not fail to observe.

"So you've been at it again, you little rat?"

As may be imagined my mood was not attuned to sympathy and loving-kindness.

"Sorry," he said.

"You may well be. Damned little nuisance. You knew I'd put you off the oil."

"Of course. And I didn't take it. When Matron wasn't looking I poured it down the washbasin."

"You did?" This shook my preconceived opinion. "Come on then, pull up your shirt and let's have a look at you."

121

"It's all better now, Dr. Laurence." He half smiled. "Let's let sleeping dogs lie."

"None of that smart guff, strip to the waist."

I didn't altogether like the look of him and while he got ready I reassembled the evidence. His von Pirquet had proved negative, his temperature varied no more than a fraction of a point and beyond that cervical swelling I had found nothing specific to confirm the presence of TB or, indeed, to account for his obvious pallor, shortness of breath, palpitation and general asthenia. I began to suspect that the good Dr. Moore before leaving for the wide-open spaces had landed me with a stoumer of a diagnosis. With this in mind I took a new look, considering that recurrent sickness, giving particular attention to the abdomen. As I had previously observed, his was somewhat distended, but this "big belly" was a not uncommon feature in the rundown children who came to the Maybelle, and I had rather taken it for granted. Now, however, I began carefully to palpate. Once again everything seemed in order, but suddenly there it was: I no more than caught the edge of it: a tender and slightly swollen spleen.

"That hurts you?"

"Somewhat . . . yes, a little," he admitted, wincing despite the understatement.

"Does it pain you when I don't press? I mean when you're up and around."

"Not really . . . just a sort of dragging feeling sometimes."

So now what? A palpable, tender spleen, at that age,

and instinctively my eyes went back to the inner sur-
face of his arms on which I could just make out a faint
purpuric staining of the skin. It had me puzzled.

"Nothing bad I hope, Dr. Laurence?"

My silence had worried him.

"Don't be a toad. This probably means you don't
have TB at all. Coming here with a false tag on you
and all that rot about scrofula."

He looked at me doubtfully.

"That's a relief. Or isn't it?"

I ignored this and said: "What else have you been
hiding, you little coward? You've had these sick attacks
for some time?"

"For a little while. But when they pass off I'm quite
hungry and can eat anything."

"What about these red blotches on your skin?"

"Well, yes, I've had them off and on. But they fade
very quickly. I thought they might be just an irrita-
tion."

"Naturally." Then I took a shot in the dark. "Have
you had bleeding recently from the inside of your
mouth, I mean from your gums?"

His eyes widened with surprise and, actually, ad-
miration.

"That's remarkably clever of you, Dr. Laurence.
Yes, as a matter of fact I have. But I think, I mean, I
thought it was my hard toothbrush."

I was silent, staring at him with ill-concealed mis-
giving intensified by this sudden and unanticipated
prospect of further trouble. What had I let myself in
for? Wasn't it enough to be saddled with his bitch of

a mother? There wasn't a trace of TB in this obnoxious
little smartie. At a guess I was faced by one of these
obscure idiopathic blood syndromes, of which there
were probably a score of different varieties, conditions
that never properly clear up, run on for years, and
break the back of the average G.P. with the need for
repeated tests, to say nothing of probable hemorrhages
and transfusions. I would not stand for it. In this in-
stance my own modification of the Hippocratic oath
was never more applicable: when stuck with a difficult
and prolonged case, get rid of it. Yes, I would put
through a couple of basic tests and if the results spelled
trouble he would have to go to the hospital. The Winton Victoria would take him if he proved patholog-
ically interesting. With a brightening of my mood, I
reflected that if he were sent home his mother could
have no excuse for remaining at the clinic. I would
be rid of them both, kill two birds with one stone, and
be free again.

Naturally I could not fling any of this at him. He
had been watching me intently as if trying to discover
what was going on in my head. Assuming an air of
cheerful camaraderie, a useful aspect of my best bedside manner, I picked up the enamel basin.

"Can't have you wasting good food like this, young
fellow. We'll have to do something about it."

"You can?"

"Why not? There's nothing wrong with your stomach. You're anemic. I'll just take a sample of your blood
to make sure."

"Bleed me? Like the old apothecaries?"

"Oh, cut out that nonsense! This is simple, and scientific. It won't hurt you a bit."

I had some difficulty in finding and puncturing his saphenous vein, which was almost threadlike, but he was quite good about it, almost too passive. I drew off five cc's, stoppered the test tube after I had smeared several slides, exclaimed cheerfully:

"There we are. When these slides are dry we'll stain them. By tomorrow we'll know all about your red corpuscles. You can even take a peep at them under the microscope yourself."

That perked him up slightly.

"What an interesting situation. A boy examining his own blood. What about that little tube?"

"We'll use that for your blood hemoglobin, and," I added indefinitely, "other things." He was obviously admiring me a lot and I scarcely liked to admit I would send it to the Kantonspital in Zurich. "Now relax for a bit. I must let them know in the kitchen about your diet."

"Bread and water?" He gave me a wan smile.

"You deserve it. Still, what would you like?"

"I'm rather hungry now after that emptying." He thought for a moment. "Mashed potatoes and," with another smile, "the meence."

Impossible not to smile back at him.

"We'll consider it. At least you can have the mash and some of that good gravy. Now cheer up. I'll do what I can for you."

I went out of the room with my own words ringing derisively in my ears. "I'll do what I can for you." Well, damn it, I would—at least I'd do as much as I reasonably could.

Naturally I avoided the office where I knew that both of my enemies would be expecting me. Instead I lit a cigarette and went into the test room. It wouldn't hurt the kid to wait for his supper, and although I had told him I would leave the slides till the morning— since I did not want him cliff-hanging on my neck all evening—I was rather curious to have a look at them.

Still smoking, I stained them, a quick simple job, and put one on the stage of the excellent Leitz. Rather than waste my cigarette, one of the oval Abdullas Lotte got me duty free through her airline, I sat down comfortably and finished it before rising to take a look.

At first I thought my oil immersion lens was maladjusted, but as I focused and refocused the same picture came up. It made me catch my breath. Although I am no virtuoso as a biologist there was no mistaking this—it hit me full in the eye. Fascinating, actually, in its own morbid manner, the sort of thing you might never see once in a G.P.'s lifetime. This was it: the field crammed with lymphocytes, white corpuscles multiplied five or six times over. I could even make out immature forms, myelocytes, large immature corpuscles from the bone marrow never present in healthy blood. Obvious, of course, what was taking place. A hyperplasia of white cell precursors in the bone marrow, progressive and uncontrolled, crowding out the progenitors of red cells and platelets, probably even eroding the bone itself. I clipped on the second slide with the measuring scale, dropped on fresh oil, and made a rough count on one square and multiplied. That settled it.

I could scarcely unlatch myself from the eyepiece. It was one of those moments, so rare in my dreary run of the mill experience, when you strike the exceptional, have been good enough to uncover it, then see the whole sequence of events, past, present and future, laid before you. The future? I had to stop patting myself on the back. This was bad news for young Capablanca—in fact the worst. Oddly enough, at the airport, the first time I sighted his sad little pan, I felt he was unlucky, marked out in some queer way for disaster. Born for trouble, out of that impossible failure of a marriage, the mark of the Davigans upon him. And now he'd had it. Still, though God knew it was the last thing I would have wanted, there was no denying that it solved my problem. I thought this over thoroughly for several minutes, then took up both slides and went into the office.

They were both waiting for me, one on either side of my desk, the brave Hulda actually occupying my chair. She looked at me uncomfortably, but with a glint of defiance, which told me they had been putting in more overtime on my character.

"Ve attend to ask what is for Daniel's supper."

"Later." I brushed it aside. "If I can have my desk, Matron?"

I stood there waiting for her to get up, which she did, though with reluctance. When I had seated myself

I faced up to the widow Davigan. That was how I meant to think of her now, or simply as Davigan, she had joined the tribe of her own free will, and after all she never called me anything but Carroll, and I would let her have it straight. She could expect no mercy from this throne.

"It's like this," I said. "For some time I've suspected that we've been misled by a false diagnosis. We're not dealing with a tubercular infection. Your boy has never had TB."

"Then what . . . ?" She broke off suspiciously.

"I've just made a blood smear. Here are the slides. They show a massive increase in the white cells. Instead of the normal five to ten thousand lymphocytes per cubic millimeter there's not far short of sixty thousand . . . plus an abnormal proliferation of myelocytes."

This meant nothing to her, but it chilled the Matron.

"You are not serious, Herr Doktor?"

I liked that Herr Doktor, the first in several days.

"Only too serious, unfortunately."

Davigan was looking confusedly from me to the Matron.

"This is something bad?"

"It coot be . . . but *natürlich* we are not sure."

I cut in firmly.

"I regret having to tell you that I'm only too sure. It's an open and shut case. The boy has myelocytic leukocythemia."

Did Davigan really get the message of these two words? I think not. At least, not entirely, for she didn't

128

wilt. She flushed up and her suspicions of me, never absent, deepened.

"I don't understand this sudden change and I don't like it."

"Are you suggesting that I like it, or that I'm in any way responsible for the sudden change?"

"It's all very peculiar . . . I don't understand . . ."

"We have been trying to make you understand."

The Matron, recovering herself, suddenly cut in.

"Who is ve? Caterina *hat recht*. There must come more advice. *Ein zweiter* opinion, *und der beste*. You must bring specialist Herr Professor Lamotte from Zurich."

"You'd only be wasting his time. And he has none to waste. Anyhow, he'd never come this far . . ."

"Then you must take the boy to him at the Kantonspital," Hulda persisted.

On the point of refusing, I suddenly changed my mind. A second opinion, particularly Lamotte's, would take the pressure off me. They could never get around his diagnosis. It must stick. And that was all I needed. I was calm, quite sure of myself.

"Very well. I agree. I'll ring up and make an appointment for the earliest possible day. Meantime," I turned to Matron, "as you were so anxious about Daniel's supper, perhaps you'll see that he gets some *consommé* and *kartoffel purée* with meat gravy."

She had something to say, but thought better of it. When she had gone I stood up, and made for the door. But Cathy caught me on the way out. Her flush had left her. She looked drawn, tight-lipped.

"I know you're up to something, Carroll, so I'm warning you. Don't try any of your dirty tricks on me or it'll be the worse for you."

I stared her out, in chilly silence. What else could you do with such a troll?

ten

THE ZÜRICH KANTONSPITAL is agreeably situated on the Zürichberg, in a residential district high up on the left bank of the Limmat. An excellent site typically ill chosen, since approaching from the river by the interminable line of steep steps, you are halfway to a coronary by the time you get there. The hospital is a massive structure, lamentably in the Swiss taste, with modern additions, offset by some tall and beautiful old trees, and to such patients as may be interested, it affords a striking view of three ancient churches; the Predigerkirche, the Grossmünster and the Fraumünster which, with the innumerable banks, suggest the split personality of this city—a devotion to both Mammon and the Lord.

On Saturday afternoon, of the following week, I came through the swinging doors and out of the Medical Department with Daniel. It was a beautiful day and as the late autumn sunshine and crisp cool air greeted us he let out a long breath of relief.

"Well, Dr. Laurence, I'm glad that's over."

He gave a bit of a laugh and took my hand, an action which, I need not add, embarrassed me acutely, gave me what in Scotland is called the grue. I was not in the best of moods. After all my trouble in making the appointment I had been hung up for most of the afternoon with only two quick chances to telephone Lotte, trying to explain why I was in Zurich without seeing her, and getting pretty well told off for my pains. Still, in the circumstances, I could not do other than let him drag on to me.

"Surely it wasn't too bad?" I said.

"Oh, no. I liked Dr. Lamotte. Very serious, with that way he has of reading right through you. But he gave me such a nice smile as I was leaving. He's clever, isn't he?"

"He's the tops," I said shortly. "French-Swiss. They're the best . . . intellectually."

"But I never thought he would send me in to all those young ladies, doing all sorts of things to me."

"Those girls are technicians . . . each trained to do a special test."

"Such as?"

"Well, more or less everything, for example, find out all about your corpuscles, and of course your blood group."

"But couldn't you have done that, Dr. Laurence?"

"Naturally, if I had their equipment. You're a group AB if you want to know."

"Is that quite regular?"

"Perfectly. It's the rarest of all the blood groups."

"What group are you?"

"I'm group O."

"They did seem rather interested in my blood." He reflected. "Perhaps it isn't blue enough." He looked up as if expecting me to smile. "I hope Dr. Lamotte gave you a good account of me."

"Of course he did," I said, freeing myself from his sweaty little clutch to give him a reassuring pat on the back. "We'll have a chat about it presently."

We walked through the avenue of plane trees, the dry fallen leaves crackling under our feet. I'd had nothing but a cold beef sandwich for lunch so I said:

"We'll have something to eat before we start back."

"Good!" he said cheerfully. "As a matter of fact, now it's all over, I'm quite peckish, and ready for anything."

This silenced me for the moment.

We got into the Opel station wagon, which I had parked in the hospital lot, and I took him to Sprungli's, which at this hour between lunch and five o'clock was not overcrowded. Upstairs at a window table I ordered poached eggs on toast, hot milk for him, café crème for myself.

"None of these lovely cakes?" he hinted. "Remember, we had a sort of agreement . . ."

"You'll have a couple after your eggs." What the hell did it matter anyway. Let him have some fun while it lasted.

As I watched his pale-skinned, tight face brighten, I looked quickly out of the window, barely seeing the heavy traffic moving in the Bahnhofstrasse or the long

133

low blue trams swinging round the island with the newspaper kiosk in the Parade Platz.

Classic leukocythemia. Malignant myelocytic type: cause still unknown. Lamotte had flattered me by confirming my diagnosis, putting a few knobs on by way of ornament. Relentlessly progressive. The multiplying abnormal cells colonizing the various organs of the body—choking liver, spleen, kidneys, lungs, proliferating in the bone marrow, pouring out more and more from the bone marrow. Symptoms: acute weakness and wasting, big belly, hemorrhage from the stomach and bowels, edema of the feet and legs from obstruction of the lymphatic vessels. Treatment: specific medication unknown; radiations in small doses inadequate, larger doses destroy the few healthy cells; in emergencies, blood transfusions. Prognosis: indeterminate yet inevitably fatal. Minimum, six months, at the most, three years.

Too bad, naturally. But he was not the first kid to get his marching orders. I had a sudden recollection of the epidemic of cerebrospinal meningitis I had come up against in the Rhondda. How many dirty blankets had I pulled over those poor little stiffs? No wonder you get tough. Quickly, I shook it off, and took a slug of coffee. The groundwork had to be laid and better now than later. When he was well into his second egg I leaned forward.

"How is the grub?"

"First rate."

"Good. That's part of your treatment—no more cod-

134

liver oil but lots of protein. I think I did mention that
you are anemic."

"Oh, you did. You were the one who really spotted it.
Did . . . did Dr. Lamotte agree?"

I nodded.

"And your treatment's all worked out for you." I
paused, then added cheerfully: "It's just a pity that we
can't work on the important part of it at the Maybelle."

His mouth opened like a hooked trout's, and a piece
of egg dropped off his fork.

"Why not?"

"We haven't got the facilities."

He digested that slowly.

"Couldn't I go to the Kantonspital? Like today?"

"I'm afraid not, Daniel. It's too far from Schlewald.
You need regular treatment. And the natural place for
you to get it is the Victoria Hospital at home."

His chin really dropped, down into his thin chicken's
neck.

"You mean, go back to Levenford?"

"Why not, boy?" I laughed. "You live there, don't
you?"

"Yes," he said slowly. "I did live there. But I . . .
Mother said . . . we were hoping we might spend a
longer time in Switzerland."

"I was hoping so too, but needs must . . . and what's
wrong with dear old Levenford?"

He was silent, his eyes on his plate.

I've not been particularly happy there since my
father died."

"You miss him?"

"I suppose I do. But it's not . . . not quite that."

"What then?"

He had gone white round the lips and suddenly I wanted to rise, get the bill, and clear out to the car. But something held me there, bending toward him, waiting for the answer. And it came. Speaking slowly, not looking at me, he said:

"When my father died, or was killed falling off the roof, there was a lot of unpleasant talk." He paused, and the thought hit me like an electric shock: no wonder Mama doesn't want to go back to Levenford.

"Yes, Danny?" I prompted.

"Boys shouted things after me. And at the inquest, after Canon Dingwall told me . . ."

He broke off, raising his head pitifully to look at me, and I saw the tears running down his cheeks. How low can you get, Carroll? Cut it out, for God's sake. You've heard more than enough.

"Come, Danny boy. Not a word more. You know we wouldn't upset you for the world. Here, take my handkerchief and I'll pop over to the counter for your cakes."

In five minutes, playing it good and hearty, I had him dried off and polished up, eating a meringue with no more than an occasional sniffle.

On the way to the car, which I had parked in Tielstrasse, I hoped it wouldn't happen, but it did. First the hand, then the usual:

"Thank you for being so decent to me, Dr. Laurence."

But when you are Carroll you can brush off compunction after no more than a brief, bad moment. Self-preservation is the first law of nature. Anything by the name of Davigan had always spelled poison for me, I positively had to get rid of them. I had nothing against this little semi-animated bit of gray matter, but the mother would kill me. Always she would have her knife in me and one day, so help me, she would out me from the Maybelle.

As we got into the car the sky had turned to a livid gray and a few soft flakes came fluttering down.

"You see, Daniel," I reasoned. "It's beginning to snow. Soon we'll be into winter and that's not very suitable for you."

"I like snow," he said, and looking up at the lovely feathery drift he muttered, half to himself as if explaining it away: "It's just the angels having a pillow fight."

"They must be knocking the hell out of themselves," I said—it was getting thicker. I left it at that, revved the engine and set off.

It was not an easy drive, the deicer wasn't working too well and at one point, near Coire, I thought I might have to stop and fit chains. But at the back of ten o'clock we reached the Maybelle.

I dropped the boy at the chalet where his mother was waiting to put him to bed, and went on to the main building. Matron, alerted by the headlights of the car—for the snow muffled all sound—was at the door to meet me, and her manner, while restrained and formal was, to my surprise, not hostile.

"*Schlechte Nacht*, Herr Doktor. You have managed

vell to come safely." Then, as I shed my coat and scarf: "*Haben Sie Hunger?*"

"I've had practically nothing to eat all day."

She nodded and turned away. Further surprises lay ahead. In my room the stove had been freshly stoked, the table was set for supper, and almost at once the old battle-ax came in with a tray on which I made out a tureen of steaming soup and something I had not seen in years—a big ashet holding the good remaining half of a steak and kidney pie.

I couldn't wait to get into it but, softened, not sitting down, I said:

"I suppose you want to hear everything."

"*Nein*, Herr Doktor." As I stared at her she went on: "You must forgive. Caterina becomes so anxious and I alzo, that I did telephone the ward sister of Dr. Lamotte. Ve know all, alas. Alzo that everything you have said of this bad illness is absolute and correct."

This from Hulda was a very handsome amende—if I hadn't been so chilled I might have glowed. But as I eased into my chair and began to ladle out the soup, she went on:

"Zo now, vithout question it is settled that Caterina and the boy must remain. This afternoon I wrote express to Herr Scrygemour telling how undispensable she becomes to me, so long without proper assistance. He will consent. It is sure. And so, Herr Doktor I wish you *gute Nacht.*"

With that she bobbed me that recently developed formal little bow and went out.

After the soup I ate the steak and kidney pie, slowly,

to goodness and the husbant zo soon dead, it is a great sin, a crime, a falseness."

"But surely, Matron . . ."

"Do not speak. Now I see clearly. She tries from the beginning to make me against you, while at the same time to get you to bed. And to steal the cognac from my stores. All *drei* bottles is gone."

"She needs a drink. At night, Matron. To make her sleep."

"Ach, it is not that she needs for sleep! No, it is not forgivable. Especially since in her haste to snatch I think she break the vacuum *Flasche*."

Put like that, the picture looked black. Undeniably there was some justification for this point of view. One way or another, with all these complex motives, Davigan had tied herself up in a nasty tangle. I put down the tray and studied the chrysanthemums, wondering how, or if, I could unravel it.

"All was in order vith us before that voman came. I managed you well. And it will return ven she is gone, vich must be at once. Yes, she must go, and with the boy—now especially that, for your thanks, he is besser."

"But what's going to happen to her? She hasn't got a bean."

"At the beginning, to show she is good *Hausfrau*, she tells me she has the offer to keep the home of some doctor."

"Dr. Ennis?"

"That is the name."

So in every way I was off the hook. I ought to feel relieved.

205

"I appreciate your . . . your kindness to me, Matron," I said. "Still . . . don't you think you should be equally generous to her?"

"Vy do you ask? For veeks you try to send her home."

"I was thinking of the hospital . . . treatment, for Daniel," I said weakly.

"Then he shall be at home there to have it, at the Spital you already recommended, vich is goot. As for her, no matter, since all the blame is for her. She must go."

What could I say? I was getting exactly what I wanted. I was in the clear. At one stroke I was rid of that nasty blot on my copybook. Somehow it did not feel so good. But I was in the hole, over the barrel, there was no way out.

"You must tell her," I said finally. *That* I couldn't face.

"I go to her directly. And you vill telephone the Flughafen for places. For the same day that we are sending Higgins and the Jamieson girl. It makes one journey for all."

She stood up and came toward me with an almost maternal yet somehow patronizing smile.

"Zo now, Herr Doktor, ve shall have goot conduct. If zo, I vish to keep you. You have skill and are clever. Zo?"

God help me, she actually patted me on the back. She *was* beginning to mother me.

I had to do it. I went into my office and rang the airport, having first thoroughly shut myself in.

I wanted no part of what might take place in the chalet although, as it turned out, there was no shindy, everything passed off in a dead calm. Zurich came through at once, and presently I was on to Schwartz, the Swiss-air clerk who usually handled the Maybelle. He knew me well, and after I'd made the reservations for the 2:10 DC 6 flight on Friday, four to Heathrow and two on to Winton by the Vanguard 4:30 connection, he held on for the usual chat.

"How is your weather?"

"Bad," I said. That's the standard opening. The Swiss enjoy themselves as the world's weather pessimists, they couldn't do without the *Föhn* in summer or the *bise* in winter.

"It will be worse. More snow coming."

"You're probably right," I said.

"By the way, Doctor." His voice took on the sissy giggle of Swiss masculine confidences. "A friend of yours keeps inquiring for you with us."

"Oh?" I said warily.

"Yes, always asking when next you are coming to Zurich." He gave his neighing laugh. "I think she misses you, that very pretty Fräulein Andersen of the Aktiebolaget Svenska Örnflyg."

Lotte, asking and missing me. It brightened me somewhat, gave me a lift, put some salve upon my ego.

"Tell her I'll be down soon. Don't say actually when. Just say in the next few days."

"Ah!" He neighed again. "You wish, *natürlich*, to surprise her."

I replaced the receiver. Lotte would take my mind off things. She would do me good. Carroll, I told myself, you'll soon be yourself again. You are, and always will be, a no good heel. It suits you, and you're dead out of character when you try to tread the straight and narrow path that leads uphill all the way.

eighteen

WE WERE IN THE TRAIN, passing through Kilchberg, and
rapidly approaching Zurich Central. Schwartz's fore-
cast on the weather had been amply justified. Heavy
and persistent snow had blocked the valley road
above Coire, making it impossible to use the station
wagon. It had been a fortunate impasse. Not only had
the journey been accomplished with that ease, speed
and warm comfort which marks the best railway
service in the world, the SBB; beyond all this, by ju-
dicious arrangement of our seats, I had escaped the
embarrassing intimacies of the small closed car. Here,
Davigan occupied one of the three-seaters in front
with Jamieson and Higgins, while Daniel and I faced
each other on single seats at the other end of the long
coach. What a relief to be spared the forced formality
of those last two days—the strained attempt to put a
normal face on a situation that might well have gone
off like a land mine. I had to hand it to Davigan. If she
had feelings she had clamped down on them hard. No

signs of distress, never a word or a look that might give her away. She even had a brightly polished smile for Matron when she thanked her for all her kindness and said good-bye. Yes, she was tough, for the past forty-eight hours she had saved the Maybelle from exploding in a battlefield of recriminations, accusations and abuse.

My headache had been the brain trust, who hung on to me like a leech. Without the faintest suspicion as to why they were leaving, he still seemed to have something on his mind. Even now, crouched in his seat, he kept stealing glances at me when he thought I wasn't looking at him, and when caught at this game he sat up like a startled rabbit. His conversation, too, lacked all its usual zip. During the trip he had piped out a series of platitudes, obvious cover for some inner turmoil.

"I must say I have enjoyed my visit to Switzerland, Laurence. It's such a lovely country. The snow is wonderful." And, twice repeated: "Perhaps I'll have the chance to see it again, and you, one of these days?"

It bothered me finding appropriate answers to his various speculations without stretching reality too far. But my difficulties would soon be over. You can bring yourself to a sensible state of mind if you look hard at the basic facts, among which I rated highly the acknowledged truth that you cannot relive the past. Yet what mainly buttressed me was the certainty that the late unhappy Davigan had been the victim of a wifely shove. Yes, she had certainly done him in. What could you make of such a woman? Sympathize with her? Feel sorry for her? The answer was a double negative that really hardened me. Admittedly she had her good points. She had guts and in bedworthiness she was the ultimate. But who was to know that one of these mornings you'd wake up, full of dreamy love, and find arsenic in your coffee?

We were slowing down, sliding gently into the station. I stood up and took our coats off the hooks above the seats. Davigan was helping the other two. There had been no need for me to exchange a word with her during the entire journey. I lowered the window and signaled a porter to take the suitcases, then we were out on the platform, following the trolley down Quai 7 to the Swissair terminal, which stands conveniently in the station. Another ten minutes of efficient service, we were in the airport bus, rolling along Stampfenbachstrasse toward Kloten. I had checked on flying conditions: the airport was swept clear of snow and flights were on schedule. Everything was going smoothly, everyone behaving according to the book. In less than an hour I would be rid of them. And free.

While I was on the way to congratulating myself I had, more and more, the strange and worrying suspicion that something queer seemed to be working to a head in Daniel. Still hanging on to me, though now less talkative, he was shifting restlessly on his seat, wiping the damp palms of his hands on his knees, looking up at me inquiringly from time to time. These signs of increased agitation began to worry me. Impossible for him to start another hemorrhage so soon.

He was full of my platelets. Yet if that odd chance came up, it would kill my whole program.

"Are you all right?" I asked him sharply.

"Yes, thank you. Are we nearly at the airport?"

The bus was now on the new bypass beyond Glattbrug.

"Only another ten minutes. Why?"

"I was just hoping we still had a little time together."

This silenced me. So far, although we seemed to get along on good terms, I had made no attempt to analyze his feelings toward me, beyond the fact that he apparently did not dislike me. I hoped he would not get emotional and make an exhibition of himself at this late stage. A quick glance across the aisle reassured me that Davigan at least was in full control of herself.

We made a circular sweep, drew up at the airport. While the others went ahead I waited to check the baggage. The head porter took our lot.

"Small party, this time, Herr Carroll."

"We'll have a larger one coming in before Christmas. At least thirty."

"That's good. I like always these Maybelle children."

I gave him a two-franc piece. You are not supposed to tip but they like you a lot better if you do.

I went in through the automatic glass doors. The main hall of the airport stretches a good fifty meters toward a glass frontage overlooking the runways. On the right, a row of Swissair counters, on the left a bank, shops, coffee bar and the offices of foreign airways.

Large as it is, this section is always crowded and I seemed to have lost my party. Then, as I pushed forward I half stopped and gave out a rude word. They were standing at the Swedish counter with Lotte.

"Well, here is our good friend, the doctor. How are you, dear Laurence?"

"Still living . . . I think."

She laughed, yet studying me closely.

"Always he makes a bad joke. Did he make them with you, Mrs. Davigan, when you were together at the Maybelle?"

"Not so you'd notice." She had to answer and she was bearing up, but with a struggle.

"At least I warned you against him. I hope he did not spoil your nice holiday. I know him so well, don't I, Laurence? Well, never mind. He will tell me all when you are gone."

Damn it, even in her bad English, she was hitting at me. And she was looking stunning, smart, better than ever, a regular Dior model, putting five years on Davigan's age. And knowing it. Davigan knew it too, in her baggy old suit, with that forced expression stuck on her face. And, so help me, I hadn't noticed before, she had on the snow boots. Suddenly I felt sorry for her.

"And now, would you like coffee?" Lotte had assumed full charge of the party. "No. Then if I may have your passports and boarding cards I will show you specially to the plane."

At least she was taking them off my hands.

"You see," she went on, "since I was here to wel-

213

come your arrival I think it is only polite to send you away."

They had begun to move toward passport control when I felt the tug on my arm. I bent down, he was pulling hard.

"I want you to take me to the washroom."

It shook me. At the last gasp, was he going to have another hemorrhage?

"Come quickly then."

I took him down the short flight of stairs beyond the coffee bar into the men's room.

"In there."

He still had my arm and he pulled me into one of the cabinets with him and shut the door. He was trembling all over.

"Hurry," I said. "Get your shorts down."

"I don't need to go, Laurence. But I had to tell you. I couldn't bear to leave you and perhaps never see you again and have you feel that I didn't like you enough to tell you my secret."

In sheer surprise I sat down on the pedestal. He came close to me, his quick breath on my cheek.

"This is exactly how it happened with my father. For weeks, as the big building was being finished, he became very upset. He always took some whiskey but now he drank much more, and at home he would get angry, even shouting, that by rights the building and all the new development should have belonged to him."

He took a quick sobbing breath.

"On the Saturday afternoon when he took us up to

show us, Mother didn't want to go. He'd had a lot to drink at dinnertime. But we went. At the top he began again, about how it had all been lost. Then he shouted 'I can't stand it, and I won't. I'll show them.' Mother saw what was coming and tried to hold him, but he broke away, that's how her dress was torn, and jumped. Oh, it was horrible to see him turning over in the air."

Again that sharp, pained sob. Riveted, I could scarcely breathe myself.

"Of course everyone thought he had slipped, at least at first. Canon Dingwall has always been our friend, we went to him at once, to ask if we should speak. He heard it all, and said the best thing was to be silent, not to make Father a suicide, which would be a big scandal in the church, but to give him what he called the benefit of the doubt. And for another reason too. There was no money left, absolutely nothing. But there was an insurance policy taken in his name by Grandfather Davigan for two thousand pounds, and meant for my education . . ." he faltered, "and with a suicide it would have been no good at all."

A prohibitive suicide clause in the insurance policy and Davigan, absolutely blameless, had taken all that suspicion and blame to get the money for Daniel's education. He would never need it now. How did I feel? It is worth a guess.

He was crying now as he put out his hand. I took it and held it. I think he wanted to kiss me but that I couldn't bear. I would have felt like Judas in reverse. Suddenly from the grille in the ceiling the loudspeaker of the public address system screamed at us:

"All passengers for Swissair Flight 419 to London will now leave by Gate 8."

"Hurry," I said.

He was still holding on to me as I rushed him up-stairs. Lotte had left his passport at the control. I picked it up, hurried him down, and through the lower lounge. They were waiting for us at Gate 8.

"You want to miss the flight?" Lotte said.

I shook hands with Higgins and Jamieson, then I had to face up to Davigan. Now that expression had become terribly thin, I was afraid she couldn't hold it. Yet she did, the effort, though, was wearing her out, yes, it was killing her. God, she did look old, pale, drawn and sick. We shook hands, just for the look of it. She had it all ready for me.

"Thank you for all you've done for Daniel, Dr. Carroll." She fumbled in her Swissair overnight bag. "It's been quite an experience knowing you. As we'll not be meeting again I'll give you this. I've been keeping it for you for quite a long time." She handed me a brown paper-wrapped package. "That morning you left me to go to your ship, you left this in my room as well."

I accepted it, stupidly, having no idea what it might be. Then they went through the gate. I stood there watching them go.

"Wait for me," Lotte called over her shoulder.

I sat down in the lounge and looked at the parcel. What was it? A time bomb? It didn't tick. I was not ticking too well myself. Anyway, what did I care? I opened it. Anticlimax. It was a book, the book Dingwall had pressed on me the day of Frank's ordination. I had walked off without it early that morning when I took off for the boat. I put it in my pocket, Lotte was coming back through the gate.

"Now, Laurence, what have you to say for yourself? You've been up to some tricks. I want big explanations before we come together again."

"I've nothing to explain . . ."

"That poor woman is breaking her heart to leave you. The moment she was in the plane the tears began. And terrible tears . . ."

"Not for me. The little boy is ill."

"Still?"

"Yes."

"There is more. I think you sleep with her."

"I told you, that's ancient history. You think I sleep with anybody. And what about you?"

"Could you blame me if I do? When you leave me so long. But I do not. That is the difference between us. Well never mind. I still like you much and now we are together for a nice cozy time. I must be on duty till six o'clock—a charter coming in from Helsingfors. But here, take the key of the flat, go there and wait for me."

I took the key.

"Mix the cocktails for six-thirty." She gave me that wide seductive smile.

When she had gone I had a sudden feverish longing to go out on the open terrace to watch the plane take off, to see the last of them, but I shoved it down to that strange pain under my ribs and stifled it, swung round, made for the exit, cadged a lift from one of the Swissair bus drivers, and in twenty minutes was set down at Lotte's flat.

nineteen

For five minutes I hesitated, although I cannot explain why, walking up and down outside the entrance, then I let myself in and switched on the lights. It was at least a relief to be off the cold damp street with the dirty banked snow on either side. The apartment was as neat, warm, and hygienic as ever. She had said to mix cocktails at six-thirty. I needed one now. I went to the trolley where a handful of leftover ice cubes were still stuck together in the thermos container, broke them up and put the gin and vermouth in. If I try to describe my state of mind you may not believe me, for now that my troubles were over and I free as air, I was sunk in the worst depression that had ever blighted me. The way I had built up the case against Davigan, totally misjudged her, and parked her off like a crate of damaged goods, would be hard to live down. For the first time in many a year I felt compunction, made worse by the thought that here, straight away, I had come up to go to bed with that honey-eyed Swedish troll. No, no, that was pushing remorse too far. Pull yourself together, Carroll, you need relaxation, a bit of fun, a taste of good living. No point in worrying over what has now slid away into past history. You are well out of a particularly nasty situation. And what could you do? You want to charter one of Lotte's jets and overtake them in mid-air, to say, please, I'm sorry, let's kiss and be friends? Forget it.

As I sat down and sipped my drink, I felt the bulge in my side pocket. Dingwall's book: *Collected Poems of Francis Thompson*. I vaguely remembered it: a nice volume, in a green leather binding, the pages slightly fogged from age, the typical prize they dish out to seminarians. I glanced at my watch. Almost an hour to wait and, in an effort to ease my mind, I looked for the poem Machiavelli had marked for me. That is how I thought of him now, beating the suicide class, because the end justified the means. I found it with the help of the holy picture he used as a bookmark—the Simone Martini favorite of my early years, he must have chosen it specially—and the title which I had forgotten was: "The Hound of Heaven."

I took a quick look at the first few lines.

I fled Him down the nights and down the days;
 I fled Him, down the arches of the years;
I fled Him, down the labyrinthine ways
  Of my own mind; and in the mist of tears

I hid from Him, and under running laughter.
   Up vistaed hopes I sped;
   And shot, precipitated
Adown Titanic glooms of chasmed fears,
From those strong Feet that followed, followed after.

I stopped abruptly as it all came back to me: the empty church after Frank's ordination where I sat and read the poem through. The incident had passed completely from my mind and now I took up the book and began to read again more slowly. The more I went into it, the more I tried to stop. This was not my line in literature and not, especially, at the present time. If I had been low before, now I was sinking deeper. But I had to go on, and when I had finished it I sat there, absolutely still, stricken and bound by its beauty and mystery.

Now it was clear to me, the genesis of that phobia, my intermittent torment, that mysterious unremitting pursuit from which there was no escape. In the empty church the day of the ordination, in a highly receptive state, I had run through the poem simply to kill time, barely conscious of its meaning, and without obvious effect. My mind was filled with other problems but my subconscious had seized it, buried deeply the theme of the sinner endlessly pursued through the labyrinthine ways of life by the Man. The symbol of the Hound had stuck too, to become the signal of release. Yes, I could rationalize it all. Somehow, that did not help. It did not seem fully to be the answer, since I, too, now felt myself *"defenseless utterly . . . grimed with*